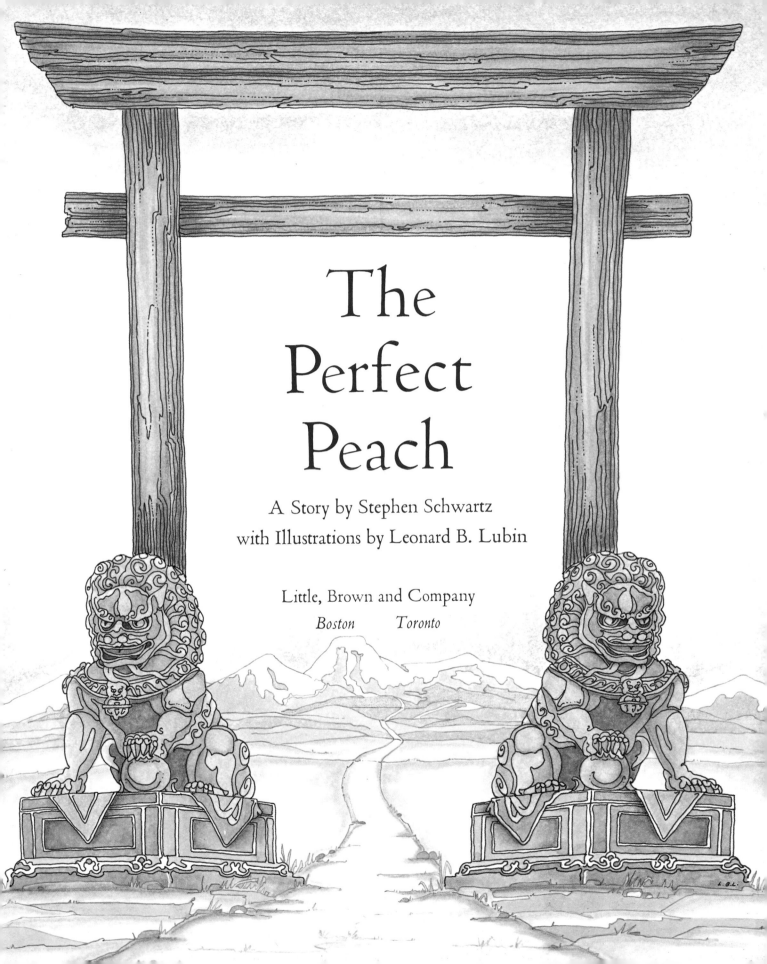

The Perfect Peach

A Story by Stephen Schwartz
with Illustrations by Leonard B. Lubin

Little, Brown and Company
Boston   Toronto

FIRST EDITION

T 04/77

Library of Congress Cataloging in Publication Data

Schwartz, Stephen.
    The perfect peach.

    SUMMARY: Chafing under the restrictions of his
over-protective parents, a little prince runs
away to the mountains where the gods live.
    [1. Fairy tales]   I. Lubin, Leonard B.
II. Title.
PZ8.S3129Pe   [E]   76-51271
ISBN 0-316-77562-2

*Published simultaneously in Canada
by Little, Brown & Company (Canada) Limited*

PRINTED IN THE UNITED STATES OF AMERICA

To Albert Van Dyke, Jr.,
and his daughter Elizabeth
L. B. L.

To my perfect peaches
Scott and Jessica
S. L. S.

When the pandas roamed the hillsides,
When the pythons crawled the weeds,
There were heroes then, they tell us,
And they did heroic deeds;
But the one I best remember
When they speak of brave and bold
Is the little boy named Pee-chee,
Who was only eight years old . . .
Or so we're told.

He lived in a great palace
As the emperor's only son;
He had silver shoes and servants,
But he didn't have much fun;
And he'd beg to join the children
As they'd run and laugh and screech,
But his parents always answered:
"You're our perfect little peach . . .
Stay out of reach."

So one misty night, as everyone lay sleeping,
Down the long and shadowed staircase he went creeping
And rode off by lantern glow
On his trusty tortoise, Ho,
Leaving early to be safe, for he was smart enough to know
A tortoise is slow.

Through the open lands they wandered
Past the valleys and the lakes,
And they slept beneath the stars,
Among the pandas and the snakes;
And they rambled through the forests
Where the trees grew thick and fat,
Till at last they had arrived
At the horizon line (and that
Was very flat).

And looming there before them
Rose the mountain of the gods,
And they both began to climb it,
Though it stretched above the clouds;
The stones cut Pee-chee's fingers,
And the dust was in his throat;
But just when they could climb no more,
A passing mountain goat
Gave them a tote.

When they reached the craggy peak, they stared in wonder,
For there stood the ancient drums that make the thunder;
And, oh, rarest joy of joys,
Pee-chee beat those drums like toys,
And he laughed to hear them booming, for like most eight-year-old boys,
He loved to make noise.

With a shout the gods came flying;
With a clatter and a roar
Came the terrible Jade Emperor
And the Dragon Kings and more,
And they bellowed in their fury:
"The intruder must be found!"
But they searched the night in vain,
For Pee-chee hid without a sound
Behind a mound.

New day! Fresh and warm as May!
Pee-chee went exploring and encountered on his way
The Boy Who Tends the Clouds (but who would much prefer to play);
They tossed the clouds like pillows, and they jumped in them like hay,
With joyful brawling.

Proud, vain, the Master of the Rain,
When a stray cloud brushed his new silk robe and left a stain,
Ran to scold the Cloud Boy, but before he could complain,
They sent him sprawling.

And all his rain went pouring down
On one little town.

Bang! Bong! Beating on a gong,
Came the mighty sun god, radiant and strong,
Throwing out his puffy chest and crowing out a song,
Bragging how if he should ever fail to come along,
The world would shiver.

Next thing, Pee-chee took his sling,
And as the boastful sun god spread a flaming wing,
Pee-chee knocked a feather off and sent it fluttering
Down to a river.

And quicker than a lizard's eye,
The waters were dry.

Run! Hide! When you prick the pride
Of the haughty sun god, you're liable to get fried!
But while sparks and cinders flew and Ho stood petrified,
Pee-chee merely laughed and raced away to duck inside
A nearby lean-to.

There, he was much surprised to see
Rows of seeds the size of melons, labeled carefully,
One for every type of shoot and sprout and nut and pea
And every bean too.

And Pee-chee tossed some down below
To see what would grow.

Snap! Crack! With her whip of black,
Old Madame Feng⁄p'o⁄p'o rode by on her tiger's back,
And Pee⁄chee leapt aboard before the sun god could attack,
Crouching where she carried all the winds tied in a sack
Of goatskin leather.

Snip! Rip! Pee⁄chee cut a strip,
And howling through the countryside, the winds began to zip,
Making people shout as they would toss and turn and flip:
"What crazy weather!"

While Pee⁄chee held the tiger tight
And flew like a kite.

In a storm that shook the heavens,
In a rage that seared the sky,
The infuriated gods cried out:
"This dreadful boy must die!"
But as they all went hunting
Through the corners of the night,
Pee-chee crept into their kitchen,
For by now he'd worked up quite
An appetite.

What a fragrance filled his nostrils,
What a feast amazed his eyes—
Made with the rarest herbs and spices
In a bowl of shocking size;
And he munched and crunched and gobbled
Every morsel he could reach,
And he ate until he'd turned into
(Or so the stories teach)
A perfect peach.

"Now we'll eat him for dessert!" the gods came screaming;
But as they drew their knives, all sharp and gleaming,
Tortoise Ho came streaking by
And took off across the sky
With the peach upon his back, for when the stakes are really high,
A tortoise can fly.

Next morning in the village,
In the middle of the square,
Pee-chee's father came to marvel
At the great peach lying there;
And to build the peach a temple,
Ninety men he did employ,
For it bore a strange resemblance
To his long-lost pride and joy—
His darling boy.

And each day, the emperor sat there, sad and solemn,
Chanting prayers, while Ho would fan the peach's column;
Till one day, the tortoise missed,
Broke the stem off with a twist,
And was just about to stick it back, when out popped Pee-chee's fist
Up to the wrist.

And his parents gasped for joy
As Pee‑chee climbed out, good as new,
And they cried: "We've missed you so!"
And he cried back: "I've missed you too!"
And his mother wept: "Oh, Pee‑chee,
How we worried! How we feared!
For the wind and rain and weather,
Ever since you disappeared,
Have been so *weird!*"

And his father said: "My son, to baby any boy who fends
For himself so well is wrong, and when I'm wrong, I make amends."
And so, as they smile down at Pee-chee playing with his friends . . .

. . . The story ends.

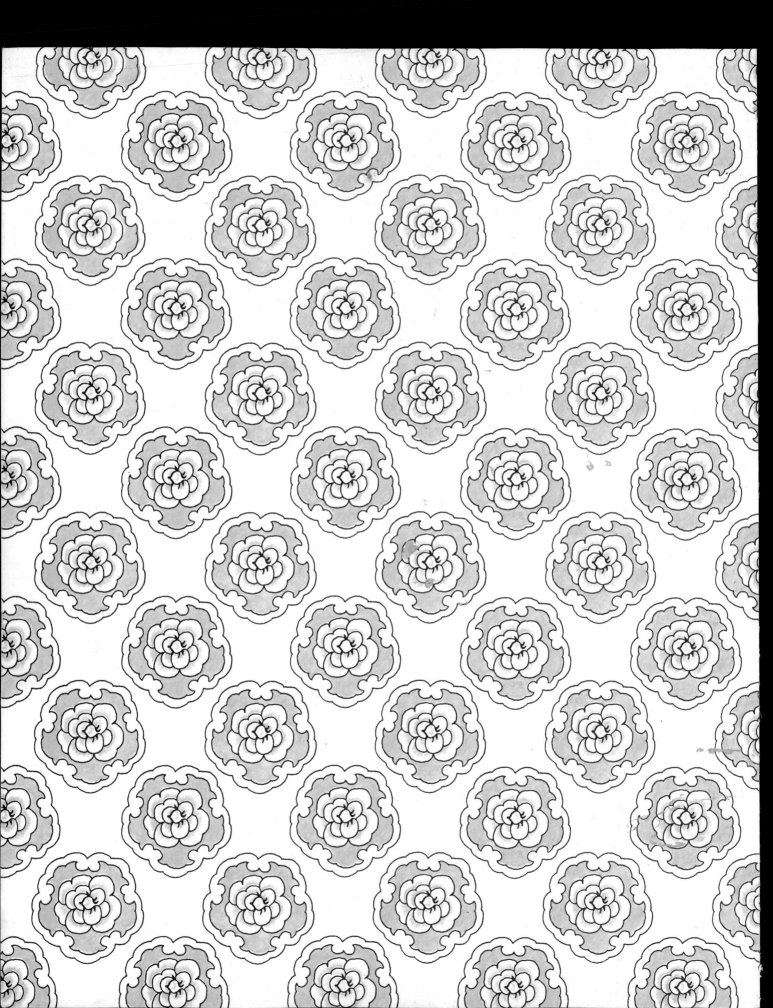